The Watchers

Terry Moore

With illustrations
by
Linda DeLeo

Bloomington, IN Milton Keynes, UK

authorHOUSE®

AuthorHouse™
1663 Liberty Drive, Suite 200
Bloomington, IN 47403
www.authorhouse.com
Phone: 1-800-839-8640

First published by AuthorHouse 9/20/2007

ISBN: 978-1-4259-8984-2 (sc)

Printed in the United States of America
Bloomington, Indiana

This book is printed on acid-free paper.

Dedication

To my wife Kim, who loves and protects the other creatures in this book: the children.

Also to my daughter Kate, both guiding lights in the novel.

Acknowledgements

I now realize, as a first time author, the importance of acknowledgments. Without the faith and support of family and friends, this book, however how well it is accepted, would've stalled and petered out a long time ago.

Kim, my wife, and Kate, my daughter, were amazingly, enthusiastic throughout the whole project, family or not. They encouraged me to continue, laughed at most of the right parts, and helped delete the others. They were my first and last editors and critics. Knowing someone liked it, even a "captive" audience, kept me typing. I truly enjoyed almost all of the process. It was quite a challenge. They say when you try to play a musical instrument, take a ballet class, or attempt to build a bird house, you really appreciate a song on the radio, The Nutcracker Suite or the house going up down the street. Charlotte's Web is a wonder to me now.

Judie Weinstein, an educator for The New Jersey Academy for Aquatic Sciences at the New Jersey State Aquarium, took the time to help a stranger confirm the information on horseshoe crabs. Her advice and expertise were invaluable.

One of my former students, Rotem Moscovich, became a long time friend, and just recently, a full time editor at a publishing house. So when she agreed to do a final edit of my book, I knew I was in good hands. I do, however, take full responsibility for any content and editing mishaps in the book.

I wrote the book for my third graders, past, present and future. Too many children's authors, in my humble opinion, dismiss the intelligence, wit and maturity of an 8 or 9 year old. Books that have vampire custodians, worm eating kids and little people running around in cabinets are fine. But my kids are eager for a challenge, a book with Big Ideas. They're ready to accept a world that has a dark side and look for a light to shine through. I hope this book encourages them to find a small "corner" of the world and improve it.

My third graders were also my biggest supporters and critics, my red pen close at hand to make changes. I will continue to read to them, if they be my only audience, and thank them for their bright eyes, optimism and laughter.

Terry Moore
3/07

Prologue

It wasn't the first time that they were attacked, these strange creatures of the cove. Yet this small one was separated from the others, and wasn't aware of the danger. Heading toward the shore it ate some clams from the ocean floor, and slowly swam to the sand. It was searching for the others. It didn't notice the humans waiting for its arrival. It crawled up onto the beach and along the edge of the water, the tiny rippling waves barely touching its legs.

Suddenly a foot lashed out at it, kicked it and watched it whirl into the air. Stunned, the creature tried to retreat toward the safety of the water, only to be grabbed by its tail and dragged backwards. The attacker screamed in pain and the creature almost made it back to the shelter of the surf.

A sharp stick stopped it, pushed it backwards and away from the protection of its watery home. And then its shelter, its shell, was turned upside down. On its back, legs waved, and spider-like pinchers clicked in defense. Yet it was helpless, unable to flip over and escape.

The shadow of the human crept over the creature and kicked it once more, spinning it around. The sharp stick was lifted high in the air and shoved downward.

A dark cloud drifted across the moon, not a sound came from the bay.

CHAPTER 1

Summer Pleasure # 1: The first day of summer vacation at the beach house! It is a day that makes you believe in forever. September seemed so faraway. Two weeks off in June, all of July and August, and a week in September.

Thoughts were barely able to stay inside Timi's head as she lay in bed. She allowed them to drift in and then float out. Good thoughts are like that. They stay there, hover around and then fly out on gentle wings.

Timi thought of the days to come at the shore house; the foamy surf, bike riding down Slinky Hill, and the ocean on a moonlit night. She turned over in bed and imagined the fireworks display on the Fourth of July. She pressed her fingers against her eyes so that bright colors would appear behind the lids like shooting rockets and starbursts. She opened her eyes and smiled when she noticed the pile of books that had been waiting patiently all winter to be read.

Waiting and hoping. Hadn't her dad told her that thinking and dreaming of something coming was a lot like smelling the baked cookies coming out of the oven? Sometimes the waiting was better than when they melt in your mouth for the first time. Well, almost. She did remember that the first cookie was always the best. Like this mid-June morning.

I'll just do nothing until September 2nd, thought Timi.

By 2 o'clock that day she was bored to tears.

Luckily there was a big thunderstorm predicted-and the phone rang at three.

"Hey Storm Girl, how's the first day of summer feel? I really missed you. It's been 10 months since I last saw you," said her best friend Sataki.

"Did you hear the forecast for this afternoon, about the big storm moving in?" asked Timi.

"Yeah, and I heard a long range weather forecast for this month and July. They predicted lots of weird stuff this summer."

Summer Pleasure # 2: Storms. They were her life. Winter blizzards, spring showers, fall Nor'easters. She especially loved crackling, hair raising, summer thunderstorms, as long as nobody got hurt. She often thought that bad weather was put on this earth to stop people from being bored all the time here.

Looking out the window she could think of no better way to begin the first day of summer than to race the storm over to Sataki's house on the north side of the beach. She threw on her favorite sneakers, the ones with the lightning bolt on the side. She was still on the phone with Sataki as her brown hair rippled from the strong breeze blowing through the window.

"I'm coming, Satak, like the wind, to your house. We can talk about your mysterious new friend and how I feel about, you know, *him*. He's a boy, right, not that I'm against boys or anything but ...Hey, by the way I missed you too."

"Yes, my new friend *is* a boy but you'll like him, he's different. Like you.

Wow, the sky is really dark. Can't you wait until after the storm? Or at least have your dad bring you over later. I don't think you should come by bike. I mean, all that metal and rain and lightning."

"I'll beat it over; the rain won't even touch me. See you soon."

Timi hung up the phone, ran into the kitchen to grab an apple, her backpack, and some cookies while checking out the sky through each window she passed. It was dark and the storm was approaching fast.

She wrote a quick note to her dad, then back through the kitchen for some more cookies, a push on the screen door and she was out and speeding down the lane on her bike.

Summer Pleasure #3: Bike Riding. Timi felt so much taller in the bike seat, the wind whipped her hair about freely and she never held onto the handlebars more tightly than this moment. She felt as if she could pedal anywhere in the world.

Why was this ride so special? This was the summer her dad finally let her ride alone. Nine years old and she had to fight to take a bike ride alone! It's not like this was the city where cars weaved in and out. This was a beach town where they vacationed every summer …less cars, less noise and bikes galore. She felt as if she could travel anywhere, see anything, with her new found freedom.

Electricity was in the air, the wind smelled of ocean spray and sparks. She pumped harder as the mile high clouds approached. Big clouds meant bright surprises inside of them, but soaking her new bike wasn't one she wanted, so she hurried onward.

She flew past the bakery, the swimsuit shop, the ice cream parlor and around the corner, three miles to be exact, to the street on the bay that Sataki lived on. The whole town seemed to be aware of the summer storm and were looking up and rushing to their cars for shelter. She loved that weather could make everybody act the same way: rushed and excited.

She still felt safe because the lightning seemed miles away and Sataki's house just around the corner. She spread her arms outward to fly onto Sataki's street, to live dangerously and to scare Sataki (and herself) half to death. Timi always believed in magic and thought she was able to make it happen.

Flash, with no warning a shock of lightning streaked across the sky. It blinded her and sent her bike wobbling, crashing into the curb, onto the sidewalk, across garbage cans and into …

a very surprised boy.

CHAPTER 2

"I'm sorry. I didn't really mean to bump into you," said the boy with a crumpled bag and potato chips scattered over his shirt. He was wearing sandals, light blue pants and a long sleeve shirt even though the day was humid.

Dazed and confused, Timi noticed Sataki running over to her as the sky pelted them with rain.

"*You're* sorry I ran into you!" yelled Timi, over the noise of the storm, "That's the stupidest thing I ever heard. You really do have nerve, placing your skinny, little body in front of my out-of-control bike. Geez, get yourself together. It was my fault."

Breathless, Sataki stood there and watched as the rain continued to soak them.

"So I see you met Brian," she said.

"Yes, I *met* Brian," said Timi, mockingly, as she wiped some dark red juice off her blouse. There were some small cuts on her arm as well.

"Brian just moved into a rental house next door to mine on the bay side on Sunset Avenue. We were coming to meet you. Remember, the *boy* I talked to you about on the phone?" blushed Sataki.

The short summer storm was winding down, just a few drops of rain left. They started walking down the street, Timi with bike in tow.

"I'm sorry," said Timi, "What's your name again? You haven't said a word since we bumped into each other."

Shyly, Brian said, "My name is Brian, Brian Delacourt from John's River, New Jersey."

"Nice to meet you, Brian Delacourt, from John's River, New Jersey. I'm Timi Ryan from Tenafly, New Jersey," she said and bowed down toward him. "Wow, so you're from here, this town. Have you lived here all your life?"

"Yes, but I wish I lived somewhere …else," replied Brian.

"I would love to live here all year, you're so lucky," interrupted Timi. "I only come here for the summer. Boy, the things I would do if I lived here all year."

They came to the end of the street and onto the shoreline of the bay. The town where she vacationed (and Brian lived) was sandwiched on a piece of land in between the Atlantic Ocean and Barnegat Bay. The bay was much calmer than the ocean: no waves, and just lapping water.

"Quick let's see if we can catch a rainbow over the bay. The sun should set in an hour and with some clouds still in the sky it should be a spectacular one," Timi said excitedly.

They walked on one of the piers that stuck out into the bay and sat on a bench at the end of it. Timi rested on the edge of the deck and stuck her feet into the water.

"Brian's dad owns the ice cream parlor down on E Street," piped in Sataki to break the silence.

Timi jumped up, "Now that's something that's music to my ears. Can we get any freebies? I love vanilla milkshakes. Hey Brian, I like you already."

Brian just smiled and looked out across the bay at the sky. His brown eyes reflected the passing storm clouds.

"What's it like living here all year?" Timi asked, "Sataki and I are summer regulars. We've been coming here since we were babies, though I only met her about four years ago. We met when our dads took us to bayside for swimming lessons. How long have you lived here? What's it like living here all year? What's your favorite subject in school? Do you like the weather?"

"It's O.K., it's a little hot sometimes," said Brian.

"Weather, but do you like all the weather, that's the main question." repeated Timi, splashing at the gnats swarming by her feet.

"Weather's weather, I don't think much about it, it just happens."

Timi stood up, swung her arms around and stopped. She lifted her arms up to the sky and waved at the departing thunderclouds.

"Weather's just weather! Billowing huge clouds are just clouds? Crimson sunsets are just sunsets?"

"Uh, oh," moaned Sataki, "Now you've done it, now you've really angered the gods. You're in for the speech of your life."

"Weather is the spice of life. It can make you feel glorious on a perfect blue day or it can make you feel sad on a misty gray one. Or those feelings switched around. A storm can keep you close by the fire on a wintry night. It can make you an Alaskan Explorer lost in a blizzard during the day. Fall without a cool wind is like an apple without the crisp bite."

Brian looked at Sataki in a strange way.

"Timi writes about this all the time. You're getting stuff she wrote in her notebook. In class we're supposed to write each day about things in our lives. Timi's entries are usually about ..."

Brian said, "Let me guess, weather?"

"Yep," sighed Sataki.

"I was born in a storm," said Timi dramatically, as she lay back on the dock. "I'm a storm child, that's how Dad sees it anyway. In fact, he thought he might name me Stormy or Misty or something like that but

I'm glad he decided against it. It would be too corny to be named after the horse in that children's book."

"I like the story of Misty the horse," mumbled Sataki.

"I was born during one of the strangest storms in N.J. history," replied Timi, ignoring her. "It was a tornado in the middle of a hurricane. There were warnings of its arrival all over the state, a really nasty one. It's a strange story. Heck, I still love to sit out on the porch and watch storms. I could do it forever. I get a tingly feeling inside when I see those dark, dark clouds approaching and know that something's gonna come. Maybe a circus of lightning bolts and rumbling thunder."

"I hate storms," said Sataki, quickly jumping in, "I'm usually under the bed hugging my Teddy, um, blanket."

"Your Teddy blanket?" joked Brian with a slight smile. "So, Timi, what IS the story of your birth that you mentioned before?"

"Oh, according to my Nana, Dad rushed out of the house that night praying that my mom wouldn't go into labor. He was working a night shift at the local weather station. He volunteers every summer at the one here on the island. So he didn't know when mom was starting to give birth to me. It was my Nana that eventually saved the day, driving through winds that threatened to take the little car and everybody in it and throw it above the rooftops. The rain was mixed in with hail."

"Now that's the type of weather I can get into, hail and snow," replied Sataki.

"Not when you've got to get to a hospital," continued Timi. "When she got there with Mom, Nana finally called Dad just as he was reporting over the radio that torrential winds were increasing and the entire city, including the hospital, was in a blackout. He had to stay there to keep giving the warnings. After hearing that report, my mother went into shock-and full labor. That means her body was pushing me out."

"That's from the film we saw in health class," frowned Sataki.

Timi was too excited to stop now. She continued the story.

"Even the emergency lights wouldn't kick in. So the birthing room was lit by the beams of a dozen flashlights. The storm raged on outside the hospital window. The sound was deafening, the rain swirling and blinding flashes of lightning flooding the room. Time ticked away. Suddenly the wind died down. It was a rare moment when all was at peace with the world. It was the quiet you'd expect in the dark hour before the morning. It was during the calm at the eye of the hurricane that this beautiful baby came into the world as still as the wind had become. Then with a slap of the doctor's hand she screamed at the top of her lungs. You know my Nana is a storyteller and she's told that to me many, many times," whispered Timi. "You got the shortened story."

The sun was setting in the west over the bay.

Summer Pleasure #4: Sunsets. The glory of the sun's last bow always opened up Timi to talk in ways that surprised herself.

"Amazing, all right," said Timi, as she rested her head on her knees. "Because of that strange and scary night, my mom decided to never have any more kids."

"So you're an only child," replied Brian, as the magic of the sunset brought him into the conversation.

Timi quickly stood up and started walking back across the dock, red faced, angry and flustered.

Sataki whispered to Brian, "Don't ever call her an only child," as she got up and started walking briskly after Timi.

Last to join them, Brian hung back and said nothing as the last rays slipped beneath the shoreline of the bay.

"I need to get home, and soon," said Timi as she hopped on her bike with a little moan, "and put some medicine on these cuts."

Brian walked over slowly to Timi and said, "I'm sorry that I said that about, you know, the only, I mean you being ..."

"Stop while you're ahead," replied Timi.

Brian continued, "To make up for it, I, I'd like to show you and Sataki a special place that not many people know about, a place I wouldn't show to many people. If you want to, Saturday night."

"I know every place, every single grain of sand on this island," said Timi.

"This place is not new. It's what happens there. But if you don't want to, you don't have to come."

"I'll think about it, but I'll have to see how my dad feels about me going out in the *nightime*. He still doesn't trust me being alone at night where he thinks vampires still roam the streets." Timi put her hands up in the air and started acting and talking like Dracula, sticking her teeth out like fangs.

They all looked at each other, made ghoulish faces, laughed and walked off into the night.

CHAPTER 3

"Time to get up for school," yelled her dad.

Timi wasn't about to get fooled with that old trick.

"Right, Dad, and you're always this cheerful when you have to go to work."

As some dads seem to do, Timi's burst into the room singing a song about good days and sunshine. She knew the song but didn't want to give her dad any wrong ideas by singing along. She was not at all happy at being woken up at the ungodly hour of 10 o'clock on a summer's morning.

Still, the day was beautiful; an exact copy of yesterday. At sunrise, the sun had stroked her cheeks and nudged her out of slumber.

"It's almost 11 o'clock," said her father, "we have shopping and wash to do, and then we can spend the afternoon on the beach, if you'd like," her dad said, "Have you called up Sataki to see if she can meet us at the beach?"

"But Dad, shopping, washing, we're on vacation!"

"But our underwear isn't."

"You're really gross."

"You know that your mother works at the hospital during the week. We do the cooking, shopping and everything we can. Now get going, I want to beat all the Monday morning shoppers at the supermarket."

Timi actually liked shopping with her dad. She was really good at it. He would take forever to stroll down the aisles while she zipped in and out with her trusty basket. She finished her list much quicker than he did. And it got them to the beach sooner-with a candy bar as a reward.

"Put some sun screen on, Timi," said her dad, "or would you prefer that I put it on?"

"I asked you a thousand times, Dad, not to even joke about that kind of thing," sighed Timi. "I'm too old for that."

"Putting suntan lotion on? The odds of someone seeing us on this wide beach are about a thousand to one," he mumbled, as he thought how proud he was that she was growing up and didn't want *daddy* to lather lotion on her back.

Timi flopped on a bright beach towel and looked out at the ocean.

Sunmmer Pleasure #5: Zoning Out. The ocean had special charms and Timi was always ready to be put under its spell. She could gaze at the waves for hours.

As she was watching them lap in and out, she noticed a group of kids walking up and down the surf poking sticks at things along the way. She also noticed on either side of them families with three or four children in them.

"Dad, I hate when someone calls me an only child," she said.

"Yeah, I know what you mean, I hate it too. It's as if they're saying we're not a family unless we have two or three or even more. You know how your mom feels about this especially."

"I know, but sometimes I wish somebody was here with me."

"Well, I'm here," said Dad trying to sound a bit hurt. His beard had flecks of sand on it, covering the streaks of grey.

"You know what I mean: other kids," Timi said as she watched what looked like a big sister chase a younger girl into the waves.

"O.K., but having an older brother or sister doesn't mean you would be having this joyous fun from dawn till dusk. You could be teased or laughed at or bopped on the head. Believe me, I know. If it were a younger sister or brother you would probably be babysitting them. You'd be complaining that you don't have enough time for yourself."

No reply from Timi.

"What about your brothers and sisters in the world? I know it sounds corny but we have to think about them as well. Too many families today are so concerned about themselves. There are others that are in need of help, like homeless kids," said her dad.

Timi felt that her dad was always preaching about a sense of care for the world.

What she wouldn't tell him these days was that she felt the *same* way as well. There wasn't too much she would tell him these days, nine going on ten. What he said made sense, but she hated it that he was the one who had to tell her about it.

"Well, then, we could adopt! I'm going for a walk. See you in a bit," she said.

"Don't be gone too long, Sataki should be here soon."

You just don't want me wandering off too far, treating me like a little girl, she thought.

She walked towards the group of kids who were barefoot with shorts on over their bathing suits. They were poking and prodding something on the beach. As she got closer she noticed that there were three boys, two girls and an animal underneath the stick. It looked like a crab or a big spider with a shell. It also looked barely alive.

"Stick it good and stick it hard," said the tallest girl.

There on the beach lay what looked like an overturned bike helmet with a crab stuck in it. It was some sort of spidery, spindly thing. Five kids had crowded around it and were pushing it around. They were jabbing it with long, sharp pieces of driftwood.

"It's wiggling," screamed one of the girls.

"Don't be such a girl," said the tall one that was doing all of the sticking. "Besides, it's barely alive. I hate these things, they're so ugly. I hate going in the water even knowing they're there. They don't scare me, it's just...they're disgusting."

Timi wandered a little closer to get a better look at the "thing." She had seen the shell of this type of crab on the beach a lot. It seemed frightened by them as well.

"Why are such creepy creatures in the water anyway?" asked the boy next to her. "I love to take them and squish them, stomp on them and kill them."

They were turning it over and over, poking it and kicking it. Timi felt very sad, even if it was strange to look at. The tall girl with red hair then picked it up by the tail and flung it into the ocean.

"Let's go, crusaders, further down the beach to rid it of crabs, jellyfish and other creepy crawlies. Kill or be killed is what we say."

They swept by Timi, the redhead giving her a brush and a stare. They went down the beach singing a song with the chorus repeated over and over, "Squish them, stomp them, kill them..."

Timi jumped into the ocean a few yards down from where they threw the crab into the water but came out quickly. She had read too many stories about monster creatures and ghosts returning from the dead.

She went back to the towel where her dad was still reading and dried herself off, thinking about what those kids had done until Pleasure #5 took over.

Summer Pleasure #6: Laying on the sand with the bright sun gleaming down, cooling off with the salt water on her body.

Timi was bothered by what she had just seen. She took out her notebook and began to write down some of her thoughts. At times, she found it hard to write in it (she'd much rather read) but dad had offered her a weekly treat for it. She thought it was actually a sneaky deal on her part since she really liked to do it. It was just hard to start.

Timi usually tried to write like a poet she liked:

"Why are such creepy crawlies in the water anyway?"
   the ocean asked the waves.
The waves replied, "I don't know but I know full well
That they're a part of things
In their own way."

"Timi!"cried Sataki as she flopped down on the blanket.

Beautiful, beautiful Sataki. Black eyes, black hair, so different from Timi's brown hair, blue eyes. No mistaking them for sisters, yet in many ways they were like sisters. The sound of Sataki's voice was music to her ears. She was such a great friend, more than a summer friend. It was wonderful taking a vacation from all the fighting amongst her friends up north.

"Hi, Sataki," said Timi, still writing in her notebook.

"How's your summer been going so far?"

"Wonderful, superb and don't remind me. Three days have passed since the end of school and there's barely 2 months left," sighed Timi as she rolled over onto her back to share her feelings with the lazy clouds.

"I know, it seems to be passing all too fast," sighed Sataki.

Dad let his paper droop as he rolled his eyes at both of them.

Sataki and Timi shifted over to the far side of the large beach blanket. They wanted to be out of hearing range of Timi's father's busybody ears.

"So, what did you think of Brian?" asked Sataki softly while drawing in the sand.

"Oh, he's O.K., but a little too quiet. And he seemed, like, kind of pale or something. He was always behind us yesterday, never able to catch up. Is he sick or something?" asked Timi.

"I don't know, I noticed that too. I was up early this morning."

"Yeah, me too," laughed Timi.

"He was just coming back with his mom from somewhere. There were no shopping bags," she whispered.

"Well now, that's a real mystery, Encyclopedia Sataki."

"No, it seemed like he was surprised when I went up to the car to say hello. He had a patch of white or some sort of band-aid on his arm. He kept covering it with his other arm."

"What did you talk about?"

"Not much and he didn't bring up the secret place he's supposed to take us to on Saturday night. It's like he changed his mind. I reminded him about it. He said to meet him at sunset by the bay."

"Ooh, very mysterious. Anyway, I forgot to ask Dad about that, did you ask your parents?"

"I mentioned it," said Sataki, "but in my house with three other kids, nobody pays that close attention to what I'm doing. Sometimes I think I'll hitchhike to California to see how long it takes for them to miss me."

"I wouldn't get as far as the bottom steps before *my* dad would call a cop to bring me home," said Timi.

"Lucky," said Sataki.

"Lucky," said Timi.

Before going to bed that night Timi asked, "Hey Dad, I need to ask about something special I need to do on Saturday night. Sataki's parents said she could do it."

CHAPTER 4

Summer Pleasure # 7: Riding a bike at night, especially down the shore.

Timi really liked to look at the windows of the cottages as she turned down the street towards the bay. Lots of vacationers would hang out on the front steps. They'd be sitting around in chairs, laughing and playing music. It was vacation time, so everybody was in a great mood.

This was a solo flight for Timi, riding without Dad. She would retrace the route she would often take with him. Faster and slower, she kept saying to herself. The wind was cool so she could pump *faster*. But dark objects and shadows cautioned her to ride *slower*. It would be a disaster if on the first night of her freedom she got into an accident. That is, another accident. Dad kept eying her arm after her fall into Brian last week.

Heat lightning over the water made her arrival all the more dramatic as she hopped off her bike like a Knight from Narnia. She almost slammed into Brian and Sataki-*again*.

Sataki said, "Eyeglasses, anyone?"

"Hi, what's up?" said Timi. "Great full moon."

"I don't like the lightning in the sky, maybe we should do this on another night," pleaded Sataki.

"That's just heat lightning. It comes from hot heat rising from the pavement during the day touching the cool air of the night."

"We have to do it tonight," replied Brian. "There aren't many days left in June but they are important ones. The moon makes it even more important to be out."

Brian looked a little like a child of the moon, thought Timi, *with his pale white face. Ooh, great entry for my notebook.*

"What is this mysterious thing that you're keeping us in suspense about?" asked Timi.

What Timi and Sataki were about to see would change their summer plans and their lives.

Perhaps forever.

Timi put her bike in Sataki's garage and they walked on the beach towards the wild part of the bay. Here the houses became fewer and fewer until finally there was nothing but marshland and bay. The bending reeds pointed the way. They walked along the shoreline for half an hour. A part of the land jutted out into the water. Timi was surprised when Brian walked into the water around it, but followed and said nothing. Around the bend, they climbed over a dune and down into a small alcove, a private bay.

It was dark as a cloud floated in front of the moon, but they could still see the outline of the shore. Brian stopped short and put his hand up to his lips to quiet their arrival. Yet it wasn't silent. Timi noticed a clicking sound that echoed in her ears. They saw a number of dark shapes moving in the water.

Just then the cloud that had covered the moon moved on and a shaft of light broke loose and flooded the bay. Timi gasped as she saw hundreds of crab- like creatures moving in towards the land. It was like a flotilla of boats landing on the beach.

What was really odd was that the crabs attached their claws onto the side of each other's shell. The lead one was pulling the one in back of it onto the sand. Timi looked at Sataki, whose eyes were almost as wide open as her mouth. Brian just stood, silently watching. The amazed group of explorers remained that way for a long time.

Timi was, of course, the first to break the silence.

"This really is a special place. The road is just five minutes from here. We must have driven by here for years and never knew this was happening," said Timi. "I've seen the shells of these things when I take beach walks with my mom and dad. In fact today some kids were…"

"What exactly is happening?" piped in Sataki.

"You're watching a ritual, a pattern that has been going on for over 400 million years. They are Limulus Polyphemus or what everybody calls horseshoe crabs. They are mating, you know, making other horseshoe crabs. They may be around for another 400 million years, but that's only a maybe."

They continued to walk down the embankment up close to where the crabs were.

"They are kinda like the world's oldest hitchhikers, you know, when people put out their thumbs and ask for a free ride," continued Brian. "They grab onto sharp edges on either side of their tail spines and hold fast."

"Looks like a whole group of crabs want a free ride," shouted Sataki gleefully. "Look, there's five, no, six of them on that one big one in the front. Reminds me of a ride I had this winter, hanging onto the back of my friend's sled."

"The female crab digs holes, lays eggs and pulls the males over the eggs. That makes baby crabs."

Timi started to smile at Brian's comments, but decided this night was too special to start giggling.

Brian walked over to one of the lone crabs and bent down to pick it up.

"Watch out," whispered Sataki. "Won't it bite you?"

"These crabs don't bite, they have no teeth but they do have pinchers to grab food," said Brian. "But the pinchers don't close in tight enough to pinch you."

Timi noticed that Brian didn't make fun of Sataki. He talked to her the way a good teacher would share some new information. This made Timi like Brian even more. As a friend, of course.

"These crabs are ocean scavengers. They skim the ocean floor and search for worms and small shellfish with those pinchers. They're like the garbage men of the ocean, cleaning up all the junk."

He lifted the crab very gently and seemed to be talking to it quietly. Timi would have been disgusted by what she saw, but she noticed the way Brian held and respected it and became interested herself.

"See the two shells. The top one looks like a… ." said Brian, as he traced his finger along the edge of the shell.

"A horseshoe!" said Sataki.

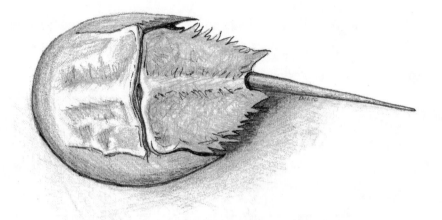

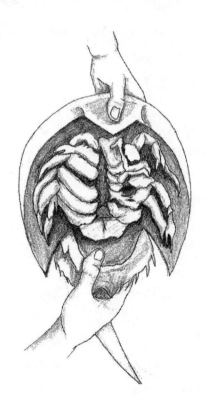

Again, with no mocking laughter in his voice, Brian continued, "Yes, like the curve of a horseshoe. It has two shell plates and here's the tail that is used like a rudder on a boat to steer it. If it loses it, it dies."

Brain started pointing with his finger.

"Now here's where it really gets interesting. Nature is truly incredible. It has two big eyes on the top to see in multiple images, seeing many pictures of you or food or an enemy. Scientists use their sight to study how we see. The two tiny eyes on the sides see light and dark, there are five more under the front rim and one on the *tail*."

"The better to see you with, my dear," joked Timi.

"It's sorta like a tail-light," chimed in Sataki.

Brian laughed. It sounded good.

Timi was now eager to see the other side of the crab. The moonlight was very helpful that night, bright and illuminating. All the clouds had passed and it was a beautiful, beautiful night.

"Incredible," she exclaimed when Brian did turn it over and all the legs started waving back and forth in the air. "What are all those little things on it-and where's its mouth?"

Brian continued, "This opening between the legs is its mouth. The little sharp edges around it are to cut up the worm when it takes these," as Brian pointed to the small claws in the front, "and shoves the food into it. The rest are walking legs. The first four raise its body up and the ones in the back act as a pole vault or stick to move it forward."

All during this time Brian was touching all of the parts without getting pinched.

"The crab is so gentle," said Timi.

"Here, hold it," said Brian and held it out carefully to Timi.

Timi really didn't want to act like a girl that couldn't deal with "scary" things. So she immediately took the crab, though her arms were stretched out, way out.

Sataki however didn't want to have anything to do with it, girl or no girl.

Timi touched it for a while and giggled when the legs brushed up against her hands.

"You should put it back in the water now," said Brian nervously. "Turn it upside down and see what it does."

Timi trusted him and placed the crab upside down in the water. It squirmed and wiggled, then used its tail to right itself up and swim away.

"Most people are afraid of the horseshoes and kill them out of fear. If something looks different, people are afraid of it," said Brian. It made Timi think of the kids she met earlier on the beach.

"But lots are killed by clam farmers because horseshoe crabs eat the clams. That angers the farmers. Companies that grind them up and use them as fertilizer to feed the soil also catch the crabs.

"So? I love to eat clams, I don't blame them. And farmers need fertilizer," claimed Sataki.

"Horseshoe crabs have been eating clams for years. There are still lots of clams. And there are other fertilizers for farmers. In fact they wiped out so many crabs that some fertilizer companies stopped doing it. No more money to be made from catching them."

Timi chimed in, "My dad says sometimes money is the reason for any company to do anything."

"But the crabs are still being caught and killed. Trappers cut up the crabs, and put them in their traps to catch conch and eels. This creates another problem. Gulls fly down and eat the eggs that are left by the crabs. No crabs, the gulls suffer."

"Doesn't that upset you, that the gulls eat the eggs?" said Timi.

"That's the natural way of things," said Brian. "The gulls need to survive. If all the eggs that the crabs laid grew into full-sized crabs, it'd be like a monster movie, *The Attack and Overrun of the Horseshoe Crabs.*"

"How do the gulls survive without the eggs?" asked Sataki.

"It makes it more difficult for survival," shrugged Brian. "They need the food for body weight because they fly in the summer to Canada to raise their own babies. Without the food, the shells of the eggs they lay may be too thin and break. If this continues, the gull population may be extinct by the year 2010. And by the way, this affects many types of birds, like sandpipers and sanderlings, not just the seagulls."

"This is all O.K., but why are you concerned about these crabs?" asked Timi.

Brian turned around and looked slowly over his shoulder and replied, "Perhaps you should ask all of us."

"All of who?" questioned Timi, as she too turned and looked around. There, in all areas of the bay, were shadows of figures, some tall, some short. A shiver of fear ran up her spine until she realized that they were all children. Children of different sizes, different colors, standing silently, watching the bay.

"There must be ten kids here just standing and looking out. What are they doing?" gasped Timi.

"They're guarding the bay," whispered Brian.

CHAPTER 5

"I was so busy looking at the crabs that I didn't notice," Sataki said.

The crabs and the children started moving. The crabs seemed to be laying more eggs in different places on the beach. The children were moving closer to Brian.

A younger girl came closer to him and put her hand in his. She wore a floppy beach hat and it didn't seem as if she had much hair on her head under the hat. Her eyes shone, her earrings dangled and Timi was reminded of an elf in her Nana's storybook.

"Why are these others here?" the girl asked gently. "Are they sick too?"

"No, Maria, they are new friends of mine. Remember we talked about letting others know about the crabs so that they can help too?" said Brian as he bent down and picked her up into his arms.

The other children nodded silently as the wind sighed in the cove.

Timi felt strangely calm and instantly comfortable with this group of kids. They seemed so different from the gang that was chopping up the sea life on the beach. She liked to be with other people, especially kids.

"O.K.," Timi said, "So here we are on the beach, in a dark alcove with a bunch of strange kids, and you tell me that you're guarding something. Guarding what? Is this the *First National Bank of Horseshoe Crabs?*"

Brian laughed again, "Not bad. That's kind of what we do. Guard the eggs, watch over them, protect them, like bank guards."

"Protect them from what, and why you guys?" asked Timi.

"The why is not easy to explain. Easy to explain, hard to tell. Maria here has cancer. So do the rest of us."

It was then that she noticed another group of kids coming up the beach and thought more would be joining them in the alcove. But these kids seemed to be walking faster. They didn't join the circle of watchers as Sataki had thought but moved closer to the crabs. They were lifting something up into the air and arcing it downward in quick motions. When she realized they were attacking the crabs at the waterline, Sataki cried out to Brian and he whirled around and started running towards the water.

Timi recognized the taller girl as the leader of the group of kids on the beach the day they were killing the jellyfish and crabs. She started whacking and stepping on the crabs. She had turned them over and was shoving a sharp pointed stick into their undersides. Her followers, four in number, were doing the same.

Brian and the rest of the watchers surrounded them and slowly started closing in on them, tightening the circle. The destruction of the crabs came to a stop.

A strange silence followed, with only a background sound of the clicking crabs.

Maria was the first to speak.

"You are hurting our friends, Rebecca," she said.

Rebecca, her red hair tangled like seaweed, said, "What's it to you, squirt?" She started jabbing at the ground where Maria was standing. Brian moved closer to Rebecca. She raised her stick in Brian's direction.

Timi suddenly felt the need to protect Maria and Brian and moved in towards Rebecca.

"Who are you? I see you have new friends to *help* you, Brian," mocked Rebecca.

"We wouldn't need anybody," said Brian softly, "if you weren't out here killing the crabs."

"Stinking, slimy, crawly little beasties, I hate them. It's our job to rid the ocean of these horrors and make it safe for human beings."

"Crabs and jellyfish and even sharks are a part of life, even if you don't like them. You kill them and it could affect us."

"You and your dumb 'save the wonderful sea life' stuff is soooo boring. We just like to have some fun and help rid the beach of a few of these nasties. We care for the children of the world too. One of these could bite somebody like Maria while she's swimming."

"You know these crabs don't really attack kids in the surf or anywhere," said Brian. "They stick closely to the bay. They're more afraid of us."

One of the boys standing next to Rebecca said in a nervous voice, "Let's go, Rebecca. These kids give me the creeps with their big eyes and white skin."

Rebecca turned to him quickly in anger but noticed the bunch of kids with her were nodding their heads in agreement. She turned toward Brian. She was only slightly taller than Brian, but she had strong arms and legs. That and the meanest eyes that Timi had ever seen; dark green and menacing.

"We killed a whole bunch so we don't have to stay much longer," said Rebecca, talking loudly enough so that all could hear. "We can find another night to do our work when the others aren't here."

"We'll be here," said Brian.

"And I'll be back," said Timi trying to sound like the action hero in a movie she once saw.

Rebecca and her friends pushed through the line of kids and disappeared over a sand dune.

Brian let out a sigh after they left and said, "It's a good thing you came tonight. With only ten of us here tonight and the others leaving, there could've been trouble."

Sataki said, "Do they come out every night?"

"The mating season happens now and it's an important time to be out here to protect the eggs. We can't stop them always but we did this time," said Brian. "Thanks to your help."

"How did you know we were going to help you?" said Timi.

"I didn't," replied Brian, "but when I met Sataki I thought she might."

Timi could see Sataki blush, thanks to a bright, brilliant moon.

"I met you in a different way: pushed into a garbage can by a wayward bike. I thought you would help because of your love of weather. That's nature too," continued Brian.

It was now Timi's turn to blush.

She laughed away her embarrassment and said, "It's late. I need to go but I'd like to meet some of the other kids."

Timi was always trying to connect to other kids.

"We will be out here every night until the mating season is over. We would love for you and Sataki to come out and be part of us, The Watchers, especially at the end of June. I have this funny feeling that Rebecca is planning something for then."

"Only if I get a T-shirt and an official Girl Scout patch for my efforts," said Timi.

Sataki jabbed Timi in the ribs and Timi gave her an "I'm only kidding" look.

Brian laughed and said, "Not a bad idea. We meet every night after sunset and try to stay as long as possible. Luckily, I don't think Rebecca can stay out as long. I know, I'm often out late. I don't know why she has to get back earlier. You should go now. They won't be back tonight."

The Watchers formed a circle, hugged, and with no sound, separated and walked away onto different pathways out through the dunes. The crabs had gone as well. Only the moonlit sky was there to watch Timi and Sataki leave the alcove. Brian remained behind.

Sataki and Timi made plans to meet at sunrise on the beach. They also agreed that for now it would be a secret they would keep from their families.

Timi jumped onto her bike as she rode past the alcove. She was amazed at how often she had passed that bay unaware of the mysteries of nature that were taking place.

It was then she remembered that Brian said that the kids had cancer.

CHAPTER 6

Now Sataki was really confused. Here she was at the place where they had agreed they would meet, the steps in front of her house. Yet Timi was nowhere to be seen, and it was well after sunset. She tried to recall this afternoon to see if she had misunderstood the meeting place. They had a burger on the boardwalk, played some video games and taken a walk on the beach at noon. They were talking about how to help Brian and The Watchers, walking in the surf and had noticed a number of horseshoe crab shells on the beach. Timi had gotten very excited, mumbled something about saucers and rushed off yelling to them to meet her in the front of Sataki's house after sunset.

She was set to go into the house when Brian appeared.

"Let's get going, Sataki, it's getting late. Where's Timi?" asked Brian.

"I don't know, we were supposed to meet here," replied Sataki.

"I was afraid this might be too much for you guys. I'll just go alone to the bay," sighed Brian. "It was pretty scary last night, I don't blame you."

Sataki stood up quickly and said, "I don't know what happened to Timi but I'm here and more than ready. I'm not afraid of Rebecca."

Brian smiled broadly, started walking toward the bay and said,

"Let's get going then. I really need you. The other Watchers are sometimes tired or sick and they're all not always there."

It was a particularly humid evening. It was a night where you feel as if you could take a shower every ten minutes only to be hot and sticky ten minutes later. So Brian and Sataki were walking slowly and talking along the way. Sataki was nervous when Timi wasn't with them but didn't show it to Brian.

When they reached the bay, there were no stars, just a fog that hung over the sky and water. The moon looked lost in a milky mixture of haze.

They arrived just in time.

The Watchers were pushing up against Rebecca's gang. Maria was sitting in the sand, crying amidst the clicking of the horseshoe crabs. Sataki and Brain started running over to the crowd and noticed that even more kids were rushing over to attack The Watchers.

They were going to be outnumbered almost two to one.

On top of everything else, Brian noticed that all of Rebecca's gang had sharp sticks. He was afraid this time that they might start using them against The Watchers. He also noticed that Rebecca was not there. He was surprised and, strangely enough, wished she was there.

When Sataki and Brian were finally up close to the group, The Watchers stepped back, as did Rebecca's gang. They then stood facing each other, Rebecca's gang with their sticks up in the air.

Just then a loud noise like a moan arose from the edge of the bay. A dark shape rose out of the water and started moving toward the crowd. Clicking and crawling, it was the largest sea animal creature anyone had ever seen. It was advancing slowly toward the frozen group of children. There were lots of white eyes and a large brown tail. It was the scream from Maria that broke the silence. The children bumped and jolted into each other, kids were falling down, getting up, and then trying very hard to get away. And get away they did at high speed, running up and over the dunes.

Brian was not running, however, just moving back ever so slowly. Sataki had picked up Maria and they were just getting to the top of the dune when they looked back. What they saw was Brian sitting on the sand, staring.

Sataki stopped, sat Maria down, and walked slowly back to where Brain was on the sand. Coming toward him was what she thought was the largest of all horseshoe crabs, with a large green shell, clacking claws and bulging eyes.

All of sudden Brian started laughing out loud and Sataki thought it was from shock and fear. It was then she realized who, not what, the mysterious creature was.

Timi!

She was laughing as hard as Brian. There was a round ski saucer (what was she doing with a snow saucer down at the shore?), painted green, on her back. Her face was also painted brown with toy plastic eyes on her cheeks and forehead. She had crawled up the beach on her hands and knees, her head just sticking out from under the saucer and had a clicker in her hand to copy the sounds of the crabs. It was just enough to fool everybody on that dark and humid night.

Out of breath from laughing, Timi plopped on the sand and said, "I didn't know I was going to scare everybody that much. I should win an Academy Award for Scariest Creature in a Supporting Role. I thought it might make us laugh and bring us all together. Instead I scattered everyone about!"

Brian was shaking his head back and forth still chuckling to himself. He too was out of breath and said, "I knew something was wrong. No horseshoe crab would do that," he gasped, "and one that size," he continued, "and ..."

Brian got on his knees and started breathing heavily. Then his face became pale and he started vomiting.

Timi came running over to him and put her hand on his back and held him up, trying to talk to him quietly and soothe him through his retching. It was a strange scene, a boy on the beach being comforted by a giant horseshoe crab. When Maria rejoined them her eyes were as wide as a bug. She was still not sure of the huge thing on the beach.

"It's the treatments," Brian finally said, "Thanks, Timi, I feel better now. I'll be O.K."

"Treatments for what?" asked Sataki. "I knew something was wrong, didn't I, Timi?"

"For leukemia," sighed Brian, his shoulders slumping.

Timi had heard about leukemia on the news. She couldn't remember what it was all about but knew it was bad. She didn't pay much attention to it because she didn't have it and didn't know anybody who did-until now.

"It's a type of cancer. Bad cells slowly eat up tiny good cells in the body and then you get very sick. The medicine you take to help you can also make you very sick," said Brian.

Maria buried her head into Brian's shoulder. Timi wanted to go over and comfort her and almost didn't want to hear anymore. Brian continued.

"There was a company here in John's River that owned a building that let pollution out into the ocean. They dumped chemicals hour after hour, day after day, year after year. They didn't really think or care what was going to happen to the ocean or the things that lived in it."

"I know," said Sataki. "We read about this in science during our unit on Ecology. Some people are really messing up the world."

"While you were reading about it, it was happening here. Messing up the ocean and our lives. We're all animals that use it," replied Brian.

"Like the crabs," said Timi.

"That's how you got sick, by swimming in the ocean?" asked Sataki.

"Yikes, we all go swimming in the ocean," said Timi.

With a small smile Brian replied, "Everybody is in danger from pollution. But the pollution that hurt us was from chemicals seeping into ground water. It's the water in streams under the earth that went into our tap water. It's the water that comes out of the kitchen faucet. The water you drink. We've been drinking it since we were babies. All the kids here were born in John's River and will …" Brian stopped.

And will die in John's River was what he was about to say, thought Timi.

"We'll fight it, storm their company. Let everybody know what's happening, and go on the evening news," shouted Timi.

"The company is long gone, the damage is done. People did scream, a whole group of people, including our parents, fought against the company. They sued them to get the money to help us and to stop the pollution of the water. The good news is that the company has stopped throwing dirty chemicals into the water. In fact, they're gone."

"Is that the spooky abandoned building down on East Street by the closed restaurant?" asked Timi.

"Yes, that's where the chemical plant used to be," said Brian.

"I know what the bad news is," said Timi.

"When the lawyers went to court they wanted to make the company pay a lot of money so that we could pay our doctors. And so that people, and other companies, all over the world would hear about the problem. We won the case and then the company said they couldn't pay any money-and left. That's the bad news. Lots of people lost their jobs. It happens all the time, my mom said, all over the world. The leukemia is also the bad news. It may be too late for us."

Two more of the children that had rejoined the group were listening to Brian talk. They slowly walked away and disappeared over the dunes.

"And it was too late for many of the crabs too," said Brian, " Many of them are affected by the chemicals, creating birth problems. That is, the ones that weren't crushed for fertilizer. And like I said before, seagulls feed on the eggs. They're in trouble too, and part of the food chain, so that's why we're here, to protect. No more killing."

Sataki had sat down on the sand with her head between her knees, her hands dangling in the sand. Next to her, little Maria was sobbing softly and Brian looked as pale as the moon. A big old horseshoe crab, looking sad and forlorn, rocking back and forth at low tide, was wondering where Rebecca was tonight.

CHAPTER 7

Summer Pleasure #8 & 9: Sleep & Rain. The pouring rain ruined the possibility for an early morning sunrise, so Timi slept until noon. She would talk to Sataki another time.

The rain, however, did not keep her off the beach. In fact she often hoped for a rainy day. She needed time to think. She loved all kinds of weather and thought it was music to her. It could make her feel a certain way. It could change a mood or add to it.

Add an iPod player and headphones to a stroll on the beach and it was magic, pure magic. Today it would be playing a combination of Mozart and one of her favorite female singers. The volume was low so the sounds of the sea and the music became one and the same as she took her walk.

To complete the perfection was the moving mural of waves, sky, and birds in concert.

There are so many colors of gray, she thought as she began one of her talks to herself. You'd need a whole box of gray crayons just to do the sky. I'd call them Grayolas.

Somehow thinking of a whole box made her think about being an only child. Not that it was ever far from her mind. Oddly enough Timi liked to be alone on days like this to think about her loneliness.

The weather and ocean were like a brother or sister, someone she could talk to.

It's not like Dad and Mom don't love me, she thought. *It just feels as if something is missing, at least everybody tells me so. Well anyway, my mom is always talking about it. I guess she feels bad about never wanting another child.*

She bent down to pick up a spiral shell and placed it in her pocket as a seagull screeched overhead.

Something is missing. Sataki always tells me how lucky I am. She says she always has to deal with her grumpy older brothers who push her around. She always has to watch her baby sister. But I see how her brother Jin takes her for walks by the bay and how baby Kati giggles when Sataki holds her in her lap.

The music became louder just as a wave crashed forward and Timi sat on the sand and cried quietly. It was a cleansing cry, one that she knew she needed but wouldn't let out in front of anybody. She didn't have the biggest problems in the world but being an "only child" was one that constantly shadowed her.

Just then she saw the shell of a horseshoe crab lying in the surf and the tears really began to flow.

Here I am crying my stupid eyes out and my problems don't even begin to match the problems that Brian and The Watchers have. How can a company be so stupid or cruel to not even know the dangers of putting toxic wastes into the water?

Don't they have kids?

She remembered that her dad told her that businesses often do things like that in poor towns, like John's River, because the people are always working hard and don't have the time to realize the problem-or do anything about it when they do find out.

Timi quickly stood up again and started breathing heavily. She walked to the overturned shell and kicked it, kicked the sand, kicked the ocean, swung around and kicked the shell so hard that it flipped out into the waves.

What about me? I swam in these waters for the last 5 years? I could wind up like The Watchers.

She paced up and down the beach for a few minutes and then sat again.

No, Brian said it was the drinking water that they think did it and mom's been having us drink that bottled stuff since I was a baby. The company shut down years ago.

Good thing the beach is deserted today or somebody would think I was a complete nut, walking back and forth, ranting and raving.

She lay back on the sand and let the light sprinkle of water soothe her face. Was it the rain or the gentle mist of the ocean spray trying to comfort her? It didn't matter, only that she felt better.

Again here I am worrying about myself all the time when The Watchers are the ones in trouble. And the crabs are being butchered by the kids and poisoned by the adults. Is a part of being an only child that I think only about me?

She sat up suddenly.

I need to get to the library and do some reading, get on the computer to get some information.

I need to help, I need to find a way, and we need a plan.

CHAPTER 8

Timi was lost in thought as she walked over to <u>Sundae's Will Never be the Same</u>, the ice cream store that Brian and his dad worked at. The rain and the wind were still blowing wildly when she opened the door and hesitated before going in.

Summer Pleasure #10: Warm, blowing breezes, light misty rain.

She was standing silently at the entrance, her face upturned toward the sky. Suddenly she felt a push against her body that jerked her towards the door. Another body slammed up against hers as she stumbled and fell through it. She turned around quickly, trying to keep her balance. Ready to yell at the stupid person who banged into her, she noticed some of the kids in the shop staring at her. It was then that she saw who had pushed her inside. It hadn't been an accident.

"Oh dear, I am truly sorry for bumping into you, dear friend. I was in a hurry to buy some sweets this afternoon," mocked Rebecca.

"You are a creep, a real unbelievable, stinking creep."

"Timi, darling, please don't be angry at me. Truly you don't think that I would bump into you on purpose?"

Rebecca's gang laughed and went over to the counter to order ice cream. Timi and Rebecca sidled over to a corner in the back of the store.

"Who are you kidding? You did it on purpose," hissed Timi, her face red from anger, wet from the rain. She realized with a chill that Rebecca knew her name.

"Big deal," whispered Rebecca, her lips tight with anger. "You and your stupid friends, The Watchers. You are nothing but dreamers that keep getting in my way. We could do more than just push you at the door."

Timi couldn't help feeling a tingle: excited over being called a Watcher, and fear because of the threat.

"And you, you're just like a boy. Always running around the beaches, cutting up animals that probably deserve to live more than you," shouted Timi.

"Some of my best friends are boys," laughed Rebecca. "They have more fun than prissy girls like you. You probably love to walk in the rain and let it whip through your hair."

Timi's face turned bright red. She wanted so badly to push Rebecca but thought better of it. What would that do anyway? She stood there, embarrassed for a second. She watched out of the corner of her eye as Brian came out of the back room. He slowly walked over to where they were standing.

"Boys love to run through the summer rain too. They're just not allowed to tell anyone," said Brian, and looked gently at Rebecca.

I could learn to like him, thought Timi.

"But not all of us hurt animals," said Brian and again looked at Timi.

Timi blushed.

"Well if it isn't Crab Boy, protector of the slimy, ugly spiders of the deep," sneered Rebecca.

"Actually, you got that right," replied Brian. "Crabs are a part of the spider family,"

"And so are you," said Rebecca.

"You seem like a normal kid," piped in Timi to Rebecca, "You walk on two legs, you have eyeballs, you like ice cream. Why do you bother the crabs so often? Do you know why The Watchers are there?"

"I don't care why the stupid Watchers are out there," said Rebecca, "and I told you, ugly things don't belong in this world. I, too, plan to keep on protecting the world from having to look at them. If it wasn't for those stupid things my dad …"

"Your dad what?" asked Timi.

Rebecca's face turned pale white and the color drained from her lips.

"I will be out there every night, stabbing, ripping, hurting every living thing in sight, animal or human. I will do this right up to the last day that they are making babies in the bay, up to the Crab Festival on the Fourth of July. There I will take great pleasure in watching people eat the little monsters."

"People don't really eat horseshoe crabs," said Brian.

"No, but they eat their cousins, the clawed ones. There'll be lots of surprises on that day. Get in our way, and you'll be sorry."

The kids who had come in the door with Rebecca had come over to them and surrounded Brian and Timi.

"Now you again know what it's like to be outnumbered. And there'll be more each night at the bay. Let's go. Michael, where's my cone?"

With a lick and a smile, she walked out the door.

Summer Pleasure #11: Ice Cream. *It just seems colder and sweeter in the summer months.*

"I bet she ordered Evil Vanilla, two scoops," said Timi.

"More likely Butt-head Banana," replied Brian.

They both laughed away the anger and the stress.

"Where's Sataki today?" asked Brian.

"She's off with her family somewhere. How did this all start?" asked Timi.

"Let's sit down at the table and I'll tell you the story, Watchers and all. Would you like an ice cream, free of charge? I have to tell my sister to watch the counter so we can talk. What flavor?"

"How about Red-Faced Raspberry," laughed Timi. "Just joking, thanks, just plain old vanilla will do."

The downpour had stopped and she was looking forward to collecting shells along the ocean on her way back and smelling the air after a fresh rain.

"Here you go, Timi, a double scoop of vanilla."

"So how did this all start, Watchers, Rebecca and all?" asked Timi, taking a long cool lick from the tall mounds of ice cream.

"I met the other Watchers at the leukemia clinic in town. We became friends.

Having a problem like this brings people together, so my dad says. We started going on trips together to places like the aquarium. It was there that we found out about the problem of the Horseshoe Crab. We began to understand that we're all in this together: animal, humans, everybody. We read everything we could on it, got more of the cluster kids involved and decided to form the club."

"What do you mean, cluster kids? Boy, this ice cream is good."

"Thanks, my family makes it fresh in the back of the shop. A cluster is a group. First there was one kid with a cancer problem, then two, then more. People began realizing there were too many kids in a small area who had these problems. Something was wrong, very wrong. Scientists and doctors began to look at the problem. They came up with the idea that the cancer might come from chemicals that were being dumped into the ocean and into the ground. That would be Dejohn's, the chemical company I told you about in John's River. They let it seep into the ground water, which wound up in our drinking water, and into us as babies when we were inside of our moms."

"And the bay?" asked Timi.

"We found out that crabs have special areas to mate and decided to look for an area where they did this. Barnegat Bay is not the only place where they mate but it is hidden. It became a very special place for us, like nature's clubhouse. In the beginning we were there just to watch. Until Rebecca and her friends came and changed all that. On that first night out, there were just three of them. They started slashing and hurting them and something just clicked in us, something just hurt. It was as if they were attacking us. All those years of hospital visits and being poked by needles and throwing up."

Brian was close to tears and Timi had enough sense to turn and look out the window. She quietly crunched on her cone.

"We rushed up to them and just started watching them, walking next to them, staring at them. We're all kind of thin and white from the treatments and that scared them and I also think..."

"What?" munched Timi.

"That Rebecca is not at all as bad as she seems, that something else is going on. She could easily have really hurt us and still can but she doesn't. She's all huff and puff. Some of the other kids could do some real harm, but I think she holds them back."

"I'm surprised, I thought she was the Queen of the Vampires," smiled Timi.

I'll have to keep cracking jokes if just to see Brian smile, thought Timi.

He continued, "She comes to the shop a lot, but rarely buys anything."

"Strange," said Timi, feeling a little jealous.

"Yeah, I agree. So we continue to go out night after night to protect the crabs," replied Brian.

"Do your parents know about this?" asked Timi.

"No," said Brian, "We wanted to keep this to ourselves. You have no idea what this is like for our parents, the hospital visits and all. I wish sometimes I could make them feel better. They have enough on their minds. They think we're meeting at the library where they drop us off. It's a short walk to the bay from there. That's another reason we like the bay."

"Listen," said Timi. "I've been thinking. I guess I understand the bay thing. I would like to keep coming but isn't there, I mean, don't you ever think of, say, doing something else? I mean something to really let people know about the problem, what's going on. I mean, it doesn't have to be the biggest thing in the world but something that just is not ..."

"Watching," said Brian.

"Yeah," said Timi.

"I think about it from time to time, but with school, the shop, and the hospital, I'm usually lost in my thoughts. Why, did you have something in mind?"

"No," said Timi as she leaned across the table like she saw in a spy movie. "I don't. But it should be on the Fourth of July."

"But the Fourth of July is when Rebecca said she would do something," replied Brian.

"Yeah, we should do something then, that's the beauty of it," smiled Timi.

"I've got to do some research on this. Read up on the problem, then maybe we can take some action."

Summer Pleasure # 12: Reading. Timi read lots of books on horseshoe crabs, leukemia and, of course, a couple of novels by Patricia McLaughlin, Roald Dahl, and the new Kate Di Camillo book.

CHAPTER 9

Mrs. Ross, Timi's mom, was rubbing her feet to ease away the tired-ness. Timi was watching her from the kitchen of the small cottage they stayed in during the summer. She wished Mom didn't have to work so much.

"Mom," said Timi as she entered the wood paneled room.

"Hi, babe, how are you doing? Come sit beside me, I haven't seen you in so long."

Timi curled up beside her like a cat in a quilted basket.

"What do you know about leukemia?" asked Timi.

"That's an unusual question, why do you ask?"

Not wishing to give away this secret part of her life, Timi lied.

"I was watching TV and there was a news report on it, about a man who was sick in the hospital and dying. Do all people who get it die, even if they're children?" asked Timi.

Her mother sighed, stroked Timi's hair and said, "You normally can't catch leukemia, it's a genetic disorder."

"Genetic?" asked Timi.

"That means it can get passed on from family to family in their genes," replied her mom.

Timi giggled, "The disease is in the pocket of their pants?"

Her mom laughed too, "Not the jeans you wear, oh you know. Genes does sound exactly like the jeans you wear, but they're very tiny things in you with messages for what your body should do as you grow. They pass good things and bad things from mothers and fathers to their children."

"Kinda like instructions," said Timi.

"More like circuit boards inside a computer. Leukemia is a type of cancer, where the white blood cells multiply and take over all the red blood cells in the body and can kill the person that has it. You don't know anyone that has it, from your classroom or anyone, do you?" asked her mother, as she sat up alarmed.

"No, like I said, it's just a TV show I saw. Don't have a fit, Mom. Is it curable?"

"Scientists are trying to find a cure and there are special medicines and treatments that help a person live longer, but these treatments can make the person feel very sick, too."

Timi just sat there and let her hands hang down by her sides. She looked at the walls of the cabin, the pictures of sailboats and lighthouses and they all seemed sad. Now more than ever she wished (if she had three wishes from a genie, all three of them would be gone) that she had a brother or sister to talk to. Or at least push around and have a fight with to take her mind off all this "dying" business.

Wanting to change the conversation, Timi jumped up and said, "Why can't we have another baby? I'd love a little sister, or even, a baby brother."

"Oh no, not now, Timi," replied her mother, "I've had a long day, your father is still at the weather station, and you wouldn't be the one having the baby."

Timi, still upset and annoyed about their other conversation, started pacing.

"I'm tired of being alone. You wouldn't understand. When you have a problem, dad is always there to talk to, you two sleep in the same bed. I'm alone," snapped Timi.

"You always have me or your dad to talk to," said her mom softly.

"It's not the same. It's selfish and you know it. If you cared about me, you'd be concerned that I'm all alone, and you know it," shouted Timi.

"Don't raise your voice at me, and of course, we're concerned about you," said her mom and slammed a kitchen pan on the table. "I will not have this conversation tonight, not after a day of hard work while you were out playing, sunning on a beautiful beach, without a care in the world, thinking only about yourself. Talk about selfishness, indeed."

The argument was getting louder and louder and Timi realized that it was also getting out of control.

"I hate you, I hate you both and I'm sorry I have to live in a family all by myself where Sataki has brothers and sisters that she's always talking about, the love they share, always playing together, caring, talking with each other," Timi exaggerated.

Then Timi, feeling sorry for herself, for the kids with leukemia, the pictures on the wall that will always remind her of pain, of how the brightness of summer seemed gone, decided to do what many do when a problem must be faced. She ran out the door.

CHAPTER 10

On a pay phone out by the beach with the gentle sounds of the ocean playing in the background, Timi talked to her father.

"But I want to come down to the station," said Timi.

"You can come down, but I won't have time to talk to you. This is a busy night, as you know. We're tracking the weather for the next couple of weeks and it seems there's a lot of sun spot activity. There could be a series of storms coming in the next month," said her dad.

"Yes, but I need to talk to you." Then Timi stopped. "Did you say serious storms?" Nothing excited her more than the thought that some tumultuous weather might be coming.

"Now don't get too excited, honey, there is just some info coming in from the computers, it's too early to tell. Listen, I'll talk to you later tonight and we can chat over some seafood, maybe eat some crab."

"No, Dad, not crab, anything but crab."

"But you love crab"

"*Used* to love crab."

"But ever since you were 5 you loved to eat crabs."

"Dad, I'm not having another argument tonight. There's no sister to help me out."

"What does that mean?"

"It means, you can just ask mom when you get home. Just ask her. I have to go now."

"Timi, this isn't about being an only child again, is it? You know how that upsets your mom."

"Of course you would stick up for her," Timi mumbled.

"I heard that," said her dad, "And family is so much more than you, your mom and me."

"I can't do this again, Dad, have this fight again. This caring for others, I just care for me tonight. I'm going to take a walk."

"Don't go too far, sweetheart. You know I love you and care for you very much. This just isn't a good night to come down to the station. Sorry."

"Me, too," said Timi, as she tiredly hung up the phone.

Magnetically, she started walking toward the beach, toward Watcher's Bay.

She thought it was the gentle clicking sound that brought her back to the bay. That, and the desire to escape from her parents, away from her loneliness and into the arms of friendship. That, and the stars bright over the water, doubling the fabric of the night.

The Watchers were there, sitting where the water meets the sand, meets their shoes. In the middle of the Watchers was Sataki. Timi had to weave her way through the shells.

"Sataki, why didn't you call me before you came here tonight?" asked Timi, flopping down next to her, "How is everybody?"

"We're fine, no bad guys yet," said Sataki.

"Have you seen Brian?"

"I'm looking at him."

Surprised, Timi turned around to where Sataki was staring and saw

Brian swimming out in the bay. She hadn't noticed him before because the water was teeming with crabs. Had she looked more closely, she would have seen a small white head bobbing amongst the shells. He was waving at them, giving her the sign to come in.

Ever so slowly and cautiously, Timi took off her shorts and top and waded into the water in her bathing suit, which she always wore under her clothes. At first slightly afraid, she now felt relaxed, as the legs and feelers of the crabs gently brushed up against her. She slunk down and sidled next to Brian.

"Hi, Brian, how ya doing?"

"I didn't think you'd come out so quickly when I waved to you."

"You looked so peaceful out there, it just seemed easy. What does the clicking sound all around remind me of?"

"I don't know," said Brian. "It does sound familiar, doesn't it?"

"I know," exclaimed Timi, "It's like the crickets I hear in the backyard at home, especially late at night in August. Right?"

When Brian didn't respond, Timi waded a little further out and swam quietly for a short while. When she turned to look for Brian, he was almost out of the water and on the beach.

He was standing next to Rebecca.

Pushing aside the crabs as gently but as quickly as possible, Timi glided through the water and headed toward the beach. The closer she got, the more she realized that there was an argument going on. It wasn't between Rebecca and Brian, but between another boy and Maria. The boy was pushing Maria around and everyone else was motionless, watching it happen. Timi rushed out of the water and was surprised to find out that Rebecca was the one that reached out to stop the pushing.

"Peter! What is wrong with you? Are you out of your mind?" screamed Rebecca.

"I can't stand the way she stares, the way she just watches, how she looks," yelled back Peter. "She's as bad as those clicking crabs out here, creeping me out."

"This is about the crabs, doing something about them, not hurting kids. She wasn't doing anything to you," snapped Rebecca.

"You can't tell me what to do. You have no right to tell me what to do," shot back Peter as he walked away. A number of the others followed.

"I have every right to tell you, I'm in charge of you and if dad ever found out what you did, he'd ..."

At this point Rebecca whirled around and realized that everyone was watching her. The children, the crabs, the moon, everyone had heard what she said. Even the darkness couldn't hide the redness in her face. Nothing more was said as she walked briskly away from the beach with Peter, over the large sand dune and onto the street.

"So, you see, Peter's her brother," said Brian.

"I guess so," replied Timi.

"And there's more to it then that," said Brian.

CHAPTER 11

Summer Pleasure #13: Amusement park rides.

She hadn't been this far off the ground since she was a child when her dad would take her on the Sky Ride. She was always afraid of how skinny the pole was that connected the ride chair to the cable that lifted them up. Not to mention how high above the people she seemed to be. The thrill however was the same. That feeling of flying as the chair came around, caught her body, flung it high into the air, as her feet dangled in the breeze. Tonight the stars shone brilliantly out of the punched black construction paper sky. She wasn't afraid, though it was nice to have Brian's company on the Sky Ride. They were gliding along the amusement part of the boardwalk, complete with bright lights and the sounds of spinning wheels of chance.

"Why do you always hold back secrets, waiting for the right time to tell?" asked Timi.

"It's just the way I am. People talk about the closest of secrets in the strangest places, eating a sandwich, rushing out the door. I don't know, I just didn't want everyone to hear about it and I don't know why," sighed Brian.

"So what's with Peter?" asked Timi, leaning her arms against the protective bar of the ride.

"He's one of us," said Brian. "He has cancer."

"Then why hasn't he joined The Watchers?"

"I don't know. There are lots of ways to react to a disease. Some people get depressed, some like to be with others, some like to do something about it-and some get very angry," said Brian.

"I guess that's how I would react, but I guess you never know how you'll feel until it happens to you," sighed Timi.

"You got that right, Timi," replied Brian. "Sometimes you go through all those reactions at once. When I go through the angry part, I really take it out on my mom and dad. I know it's tough on them too, but then I disappear for periods of time, escaping to different places, sometimes going for long walks without letting them know, going to The Watcher's place.

"I also sulk and hope that they feel bad and come and try to help or comfort me. It's like my parents are not the ones to blame, but they're the only ones I can attack and know, I guess, that they won't turn around and leave me. I get angry at my sister too."

"I didn't know you had a sister," said Timi.

"Yes, don't you remember, she works at the ice cream store too? She's really nice to me, too nice. Still, sometimes I can treat her mean and I get away with it because of the cancer. No one yells at me. I hate myself when that happens."

"You hate yourself?" asked Timi.

"Yeah, I think I'd rather be punished then treated so special."

"This is so cool, Brian, floating above the people on the Sky Ride, and the night is so calm. I bet we could listen in on what people were saying if we were quiet enough. There are so few people on the board-walk tonight. And no one will even notice we're snooping," whispered Timi. "I love nights like this, nights without any weather. It's like the rain, the moon and the wind are taking a day off."

It was indeed an unusually windless night for this part of the shore and this part of the boardwalk had no arcades or amusement rides. You could practically hear what the dolphins were singing.

"Let's pretend we're guardian angels and here tonight to float over and listen in. Oooh, I can hear what those two girls are saying," said

55

Timi excitedly. Brian leaned over to pay attention as well.

They listened intently for ten minutes, then turned their heads towards each other and laughed.

"So much for being a guardian angel," said Brian "We spent the whole time hearing an argument over which eye make-up looked good on Wednesday night and which kind looked better on a Thursday."

"Maybe we should've helped them to *make up*, get it Brian?" said Timi. Brian made a face.

Timi looked down. "Look, over there's a man with his wife and three kids. I bet they're having a great time."

"OK," said Brian, "Let's see if you're right. And no more bad jokes."

Again they leaned over and listened for a short time as the cable car hung suspended over the family. Timi tucked her arms under her armpits to imitate an angel hovering over. Brian laughed.

Timi had a look of surprise on her face after they passed the family. Later she turned towards Brian and said, "So I guess this guardian angel can be wrong. The two little boys were the dad's and the one older girl was the mom's. I thought they were one big happy family. They seemed very uncomfortable with each other. Lots of arguing. Maybe the parents are divorced."

"Deciding which parent to be with after a divorce must be a really tough decision to make," said Brian.

"I guess having a big family doesn't always mean happy-or easy," mumbled Timi.

"Hey, look who's walking right ahead," murmured Brian.

"Where, who are you pointing at?" asked Timi.

"Over by the pizzeria, the girl with the man," replied Brian.

"Oh my God, it's Rebecca," gasped Timi.

"Yes, Rebecca, and who? Let's listen in, Angel Gabriel."

As they watched, Rebecca kept moving away from the man. He seemed to be weaving in and out on the boardwalk, swaying as he strolled. They were clearly arguing and Rebecca was in tears. Timi and Brian flew silently over the whole scene, fearful of making any sound that might alert them that they were above them. After passing, they remained silent until they slid off the ride.

"So that explains why Rebecca's been so angry about the crabs," said Brian finally.

"Yes, her father made his living off of them, that's why he kept yelling about the crabs that ruined his life," said Timi.

"He was really loud, wasn't he?" added Brian, "and very drunk."

"My guess is he's one of those crabbers that sell them to farmers for the fertilizer. They crush the crabs and put it in the soil to enrich the crops. There are new laws that limit the amount of crabbing in this area, so it put her father out of a job."

"That would explain Rebecca's anger toward the crabs and her brother's anger with the group," said Timi. "What a mess for Rebecca: your dad not working and your brother with cancer."

"But why did her father have to keep hitting her?" yelled Brian, as he pounded his fist on the beach railing.

"Maybe some families work out their problems, like the one we saw in the middle of the ride, and some take it out on whoever's around, even your own daughter," sighed Timi.

"It makes me think again about my sister and family and how I treat them when I'm angry about the chemotherapy."

"What's chemotherapy?" asked Timi.

"It's where they shoot poisonous chemicals into your bloodstream to kill the cancer. Unfortunately, it hurts other parts of your body too. It's like aspirin. When I was little I wondered how aspirin knew where the pain was, like in your head for a headache. It doesn't. It affects other parts of the body. The chemical to stop the cancer attacks other parts of my body and also makes me sick."

"So that's what makes you look pale all the time?" asked Timi.

"That and your bad jokes. See you tomorrow night at the bay. You are coming, aren't you? Luckily, there were enough of the others to watch the bay so we could take tonight off and have some fun on the boardwalk and be hovering angels," said Brian.

"It was a great idea. I really enjoyed it. And like the girls on the boardwalk, I won't *make-up* any more bad jokes."

Brian just moaned.

CHAPTER 12

Timi and Brian weren't at the bay the whole night, or the ice cream parlor, or the boardwalk. They were at the police station. Peter was in the hospital in a coma, and Rebecca and Timi were screaming at each other.

"Quiet down, quiet *down*," said the officer with the kind but concerned face standing in between the two girls, "Let's hear both sides of the story. No one is being accused of anything yet. Your parents have been called and they'll be here in a minute. This is a serious thing that happened and we need to get to the bottom of this."

Rebecca blurted out first, "This jerk, Timi, pushed my brother down onto a rock, smashed his head open, and now he's in the hospital. There's not much more to say. She's a murderer and you should put her in jail now!" Her face was as white as the neon lights that buzzed from the ceiling.

Timi, flushed in the face, tears streaming down her cheeks, sat on a nearby bench. The police station was bright, clean, and quiet, unlike the station houses she had seen on TV. People weren't running about, there weren't any hardened criminals, and the officers seemed nice to them.

"I didn't mean to hurt Peter. I came to meet Brian and some friends. We hang out at the bay sometimes to watch the horseshoe crabs. Rebecca and some friends came to… watch, too and Peter got in a fight with the other girl, Maria, and started pushing her around. I, I stepped in to stop it and started yelling at Peter and moving toward him and he kept moving backward and backward up by the sand dune and the next thing I knew he fell backward and was quiet."

Timi was so upset that she didn't notice that her parents had walked in and were listening to the story by the door.

Rebecca continued, "That's a lie, a bold-faced lie. I saw you push him into the rock, right into the big, black rock and now Peter is in a coma because of you."

Timi's mom walked next to Timi and sat down and put her arms around her. Timi continued to talk through the sobs.

"I didn't see any rock. I didn't want to hurt Peter; I just wanted to stop him. I was the first to go running over the dune to wave at that car. They called the ambulance that took Peter to the hospital and Maria as well. That was Peter's fault."

"Peter did *nothing*," countered Rebecca, "He was just talking to her."

At this point, both Rebecca and Timi kept shouting at each other until the officer put his hands up and said, "Are you the parents of Timi or Rebecca?"

Timi's dad went over and shook the hand of the officer and said quietly, "I'm Mr. Ross, and this is my wife, Mrs. Ross. We're Timi's parents."

"I'll need to get a statement from your daughter, Timi, in a minute, after I get a statement from Rebecca. Rebecca, your dad is at the hospital, and another officer will drive you over the minute we're finished."

Rebecca sat down on the bench as Timi and her family went to the back of the station. Rebecca looked alone and small next to the large police desk.

"I'm in all the newspapers, I'm a regular criminal," sobbed Timi, as she sat in the back of the ice cream store next to the empty containers of lemon sherbert stacked on the shelves behind her. Brian was sitting next to her, listening closely.

"Well, it's just the local ones. Nobody outside of John's River will know," said Brian.

"No way, one of my classmates from up north read about it and called me. She thought it was real cool, wanted to know what it was like to be in a jail cell."

"You weren't in a jail cell and you were released to your parents to…"

"Go ahead and say it, to go to court later on. Can you imagine, me, going to court? I'm frightened to let my library books stay out one day over the time limit. I won't even sneak my friends into the community pool. Now I'm a New Jersey Mafia gangster. And reporters have been calling the house all day."

The trickle of tears turned into a stream at this point, although Timi did everything possible to stem the flow. Brian, on the other hand, did everything possible not to put his arm around her to comfort her, much as he wanted to help. Instead it hung over a dusty box.

"Everything will be cleared up, everything will work out, you'll see," smiled Brian. "It was dark the night everything happened; even I couldn't see what was going on. How can you be accused of a crime that no one could see?"

Timi stopped crying and was silent for a minute. She got up from the carton she was squatting on and stood over in a corner of the stock room and said quietly, "I did hurt Peter. I wanted to. It wasn't an accident."

Brian was quiet for a moment and replied, "You couldn't have intentionally tried to hurt Peter in that way?"

"See, even you're not sure of me. I did want to hurt him, I was incredibly angry, sick of all this crab nonsense and he was really scaring Maria, telling her he was going to throw her in the bay and watch all the crabs eat her up. That's when she fainted. He started moving backwards and I tripped him, you know the type of thing you see in karate movies, I didn't think it would work. When he fell on the sand, I was glad. When I realized it was a rock, I panicked."

Brian stared up at her.

"Then I realized what a horrible thing I had done. He was breathing heavy and there was blood on his hair. I started running toward the street to get help."

It was dark in the back storeroom, though the morning was bright with sunlight.

"That part I remember," said Brian. "You were like a banshee hollering at every car that passed by."

"How are Maria… and Peter? Oh what a mess this is."

"Peter is still in a coma, Maria is on intravenous medication. You didn't hurt Peter on purpose any more than he meant to send Maria to the hospital. Both were accidents because of your anger, but *accidents.*"

The cloud that had been blocking the sun passed over and bright sunlight slanted through the window, reflecting on the side wall.

Timi put her hands up to her face and quietly cried, but this time it sounded now more like a sigh of release from the guilt and fear.

"What am I going to do?"

"I've been thinking about that," said Brian, "about what you said about your classmate hearing about it in North Jersey. When life gives you lemons, make lemonade."

"Great, I'm going to jail, you're thinking about citrus fruit."

Brian stood up, and started pacing from the back door to the far wall.

"I think you should tell your story to the papers. The whole story. You said reporters are calling every day; well this is a perfect opportunity to tell everyone your side of the story-our story. Get out the facts about the toxic chemicals being dumped into the ocean, about the plight of the crabs."

"But what if I tell the whole story, the true story?" cried Timi.

"You didn't really mean to hurt Peter the way you did," soothed Brian.

Timi didn't reply.

CHAPTER 13

The hospital room reeked of odors that Timi didn't like. The wax smell on the floors, the disinfectants and the medications. It was worse than the way the school smelled in September. She was standing by Maria's bed and all these tubes were in her nose and arms. Sounds vibrated as the machines clicked and hummed. *Well, if nothing else,* thought Timi, *I'm learning a lot about the real world outside of TV, with police stations, hospitals, leukemia- and I don't like it.*

Maria was quiet, pale and wan under the sheets, and Timi wished Brian had not left her alone to go for a soda. What if Maria woke up? What would she say to her? "How ya doin? What do you think of those Yankees?"

Well, she wasn't going to stand by the bed alone, so she started walking down the children's ward, lost in thought.

Days had passed and things were beginning to look up. Peter seemed to be coming out of his coma.

"Peter will be out of his coma and Maria is just sleeping, her medicine just knocked her out," she whispered aloud to reassure herself that everything was going to be OK.

The major newspapers had picked up the interview she had with the shore reporter and it had been printed in the *John's River Herald* newspaper. In the story she talked about The Watchers, the toxicity in the ocean, the horseshoe crabs, everything. She was not allowed to talk about the accident until her court case, so she didn't, but she thought lots of people might be able to read between the lines and figure out that she was trying to protect. .. protect what? The crabs or Maria? Her friendships?

As she walked, she saw Peter in one of the rooms. Actually, she knew he was somewhere in the hospital and had wandered about in hope of finding this very room. She wanted to go in to apologize, to say something to Peter about what had happened. Inside the room was a doctor looking over Peter's chart. He was smiling and looking over a peaceful, sleeping Peter. Suddenly something inside of Timi tingled and she felt she needed to know something about what was happening to Peter. She waited in the hallway for the doctor to finish and started talking to him as he came out of the room. He recognized Timi as the girl in the newspaper and knew all about what had happened. He started talking to her as her face went from confused, to smiling, to surprise and astonishment as she opened her mouth and put her hand in front of it. She thanked the doctor for what seemed like a thousand times and started toward the elevator. Timi couldn't wait to tell Brian, Sataki and all The Watchers what she had learned, and especially Rebecca.

Outside the hospital, a confused Timi decided to stroll down the beach and let the ocean surf, the sea gulls and the wind be her music as she tried to sort out her confusion. *It's good Peter is better and the news from the doctor is really good. Maria is improving but may need to be flown to a special hospital for treatments.* She should be happy with the news but wasn't and started crying.

Maria is still sick, why can't I do anything about it? It's so unfair that this is happening to her.

The tears started rolling out again.

Or am I sad because I'm scared that leukemia could happen to me and am glad that it's not me? I feel so helpless. The companies poisoned the water and just turned around and left. How can I do anything to stop it? These people are like criminals. No, they are criminals, just like the bad guys I watch on TV. Only worse cause they killed lots of people and got away with murder.

I don't have anybody to talk to; my sister may as well be my reflection in the mirror in my room.

As she was walking, Timi noticed a family in the distance playing by the jetty jutting into the ocean.

They are so lucky to have each other, she thought.

Timi was about to sit down to have a cry that would add an inch of water to the ocean, when she heard shouts from down the beach. She quickly wiped the teardrops from her cheeks, and turned around to show her brave face.

It was Brian and Sataki. What a sight for sore eyes!

Out of breath, Sataki put her arm around Timi and started wise-cracking immediately, "Hey, you having one of your moody, quiet walks along the beach? Are you trying to save the world again by thinking it through?"

Nothing like having friends to kid you out of your dark feelings, thought Timi and laughed out loud at Sataki's gentle teasing. All along Sataki had been with her, comforting her after she came home from the court-house. She called her on the phone and took many bike rides and ocean swims with her.

Brian looked at Timi and noticed the redness in her eyes and asked, "How are you Timi? Are you thinking about your court case?"

"Oh no, not the court case. I nearly forgot about it," Timi sighed,

"I was thinking about Maria and the crabs and DeJohn's factory." She didn't mention her thoughts about how relieved she was to not have leukemia, especially to Brian.

"We were talking about that too and we have an idea," piped in Sataki.

"Go, ahead, I'm all ears," said Timi, and was about to make a joke about elephants but instead said, "I'm listening."

Sataki continued, clearly excited, "Remember your idea about doing something on the same day as Rebecca plans to do something at the Crab Festival on the 4th of July? Well, Brian and I thought we could do a teach-in. My dad says that's when you teach people about something, like a class. But it doesn't have to be in a classroom. We can use charts, graphs, and stuff from the Internet. We can teach them about horseshoe crabs and ocean pollution and everything."

Brian added, "I can stop at the aquarium in Camden. There's a curator there who's given me a lot of information on the crabs and I can get even more, maybe even some pictures."

Timi was caught up in the excitement as well and said, "Dad has some information down at the weather station and knows other people in oceanography that might be able to help us."

Soon, the talk was overflowing with their arms waving, laughing and the making of plans, plans, plans.

"We've really got to get moving," said Timi, "That festival is soon and we've got a lot of work to do."

Each of them took an assignment and headed their separate ways. Timi wanted a little more time to walk on the beach and think. As she was wading through the shallow part of the tide line, she wiggled her toes, causing ripples in the water. The smooth motion of those little waves continued all the way to the shore. She looked up and also noticed the larger undulating ocean waves that had started so far out and continued to flow toward the beach. That word, ripple, kept coming up in her mind, how things have a ripple effect, one thing causing another thing, causing another. She could sense that a storm was brewing that would blanket the area with thunder and lighting and at the same time create great waves of change in their lives. She was proud to be a part of it, excited to have done something to make it happen. She felt electric.

It was then that she remembered that she forgot to tell Sataki and Brian about the doctor and her special news.

CHAPTER 14

Summer Pleasure #14: Anticipation. *Sometimes, it's better waiting for what happens than what actually happens,* thought Timi, looking up at the sky, *at least that's what dad always says. But I just can't wait for this storm to come. They've been predicting it for days and it looks like it going to be a doozy.*

The sky was indeed dark and moody, allowing no light-not even a hint-to shine through. There was an abundance of static electricity in the air causing the hair on the back of her neck to stand up. She noticed dust devils dancing in the sand as she walked parallel to the beach.

Timi was walking briskly along Ocean Boulevard, heading toward the entrance to Seaside Beach, where the Crab Festival was being held. Timi was to meet Sataki and Brian there. They all had had a busy week. All had done more than their share of the research, gathered the information and made charts and signs. They had thought of a computer slide presentation but were afraid that the light on the beach would make it impossible to see. Sataki even had made a sculpture of a horseshoe crab out of plaster with her sister's help. But under Timi's arm was the most important chart of all, the one that would surprise everyone, including The Watchers.

All up and down a two block radius, colorful festival signs were flapping furiously in the wind. There were giant crab balloons, fuzzy small stuffed ones, edible real ones on hamburger buns, even blue crab ice cream at one of the stands. I hope Brian's dad doesn't start selling that at his store, thought Timi. She was looking for the stand the town committee had allowed them to set up for their teach-in.

"Where have you been?" cried Sataki, waving her over to their stand. Brian, Sataki and a couple of The Watchers were in the space behind the table.

"I didn't think it would get this crowded by 2 o'clock," said Timi.

"It just started to really get packed about 15 minutes ago," replied Brian. "I think people are afraid that the storm is coming in quicker than was predicted."

"Yeah, even my dad was surprised." said Timi. "The stand looks great. The pictures really came out cool, and so did your crab."

Sataki held a stuffed horseshoe crab in her hand. Then in a gravelly voice she growled, "Hi, my name is Helmet, the gentle horseshoe crab. Please don't eat me; I'm a special kind of crab.'

"I don't know how anybody can eat *any* kind of crab," said Timi. "I used to like them but now I don't. They're caught and boiled, actually tortured."

"We can only change one corner of the world at a time," interrupted Brian, "so let's get busy convincing people how to help the horseshoes."

"That's OK with me," grumbled Helmet, and everybody laughed at small Sataki's strange low voice.

For the rest of the afternoon, things went along swimmingly. Many people approached the booth, took the flyers they had printed up and asked lots of questions about the crabs. Most people didn't know about the problem and were genuinely concerned and wanted to help. There were a few who shrugged their shoulders and seemed not to care, but mostly everybody appreciated the information and many signed a petition asking that there be action taken to protect the crabs.

The weather was not as helpful or appreciative. It got darker and darker as the day diminished. Timi couldn't be more thrilled. Not so for Sataki.

"I hope you got everything ready to pack up and leave quickly. Those cumulonimbus clouds are really black at the bottom," said Timi.

"I don't care what you call them, I thought I heard thunder in the distance. I think it's time to go," Sataki said nervously.

At that moment lightning flashed across the sky and Timi started counting the number of seconds to calculate how far away the storm was.

"Eight, nine, ten," and at that moment a large clap of thunder boomed across the sky. Rebecca strode through the crowd and stood in front of the shocked Watchers. The wind was whipping her hair, she was laughing like a witch. Hanging from her outstretched arm was what was left of a mangled horseshoe crab.

CHAPTER 15

Timi looked at Sataki and realized why the rest of Rebecca's gang was not there.

"They're slaughtering the horseshoes; it's a mass killing, that's what Rebecca had planned- to rid the beach of all the crabs. The fact that we're at the festival just made it easier for them!" shouted Timi to Brian and Sataki.

The wind was picking up; festival goers were dispersing as the clouds thickened. Timi started running toward the bay with the other Watchers in tow. As she ran off the beach towards the bay, she noticed her parents were walking onto the beach and yelled to them where she was going. The wind was quite violent now; the sea and the sand were swirling around.

Lightning flashed and raced along with Timi, but she felt much faster, knowing she had to reach the bay to stop the killing. She counted the seconds before the next clap of thunder and only got to two. The storm was upon them. Timi leapt over the dunes and stopped, staring transfixed on the scene in front of her. Many of the crabs were dead, strewn across the beach. Sticks were raised in the air like a Flag Day parade and were cracking down on the shells. Many of the crabs were upside down, their tails no longer able to turn themselves over. Some were without tails at all.

"It's our final battle," jeered Rebecca, and Timi jumped around to see her twisted face.

Timi started to run toward the massacre and Rebecca grabbed her by the hair and yanked her back.

Timi swung at her, but the quick turn around tossed her in the sand. She got up slowly, as Rebecca watched her every move with clenched fists.

"These *crabs* are why my dad's being laid off. These *crabs* are why he gets drunk every night and then hits me. These *crabs* are ruining our lives."

"Rebecca, you don't get it, you just don't understand. They *saved* your brother's life!"

"What are you talking about?" shouted Rebecca as she took a few steps backward. The rest of The Watchers came over the dunes, stopped, and then ran past Rebecca and Timi. They moved down by the water's edge, encircled Rebecca's gang and momentarily, the killing stopped. One of The Watchers looked around at the bloodshed and vomited.

Timi's mom and dad and a number of parents who followed were now at the crest of the hill overlooking the bay. Lighting flashed regularly now, no longer patient to wait for the thunder. All the killing had stopped and all the children were gathered around Rebecca and Timi.

Timi shouted above the chaos, "The crab's blood is used as a test in the hospital to ensure that certain medicines that are put in a patient's body are safe. It's called Methylene Blue. They found out that some untested drug accidentally caused your brother's infection. His coma had nothing to do with his fall. Now that the doctors know what the problem is, they can help him, thanks to Methylene Blue. That's what saved your brother-the blood of the horseshoe crab."

"That's impossible," shouted Rebecca, above the rain and thunder. "How can they do that, how do you know so much about it? And it would kill your precious crabs."

"The doctor that treated your brother told me all about it. Then I went to the library and looked it up. Only a little blood is used. It doesn't hurt the crab. Your brother's out of the coma and will be fine."

"Another lie. My brother is still in a coma," cried Rebecca.

"He was probably sleeping when you went into the hospital room. One of The Watchers who's been in the hospital told me a little while ago at the crab booth. You ran out before you could find out. You were so busy rushing to kill the crabs that you didn't take the time to find out," yelled Timi.

The lightning and the thunder were now mixed together in a terrible storm stew.

"Don't you get it?" Timi shrieked, twisting around, into Rebecca's face. "We're all in this together. Without the crabs, there might be too much garbage on the ocean floor. Bird populations could become extinct. Patients might die of bad medicine. We need to care, to *watch out* for each other. We can't survive without each other. You, me, The Watchers, everyone..."

Timi's parents walked down the hill and threw a poncho on Timi's back. Her dad murmured, "So this is where you've been all these nights. I knew something was up."

Rebecca slumped on her knees and started sobbing. Timi's mom put an umbrella over her, picked her up and they all silently walked over the dunes and toward the cars. Timi and Rebecca stopped together at the top and took one last look as a single lightning bolt crashed into the bay. Some crabs were finally stirring and swimming back into the cove.

A few days later, Brian, Sataki and Timi were standing on the beach looking out over the bay, recounting the events of the last couple of days. The beach was empty of crabs now that the mating season was over. Maria was gone, flown away to another special hospital to help her get better. Rebecca had gone to the police and told them that Peter's fall wasn't Timi's fault, that it was an accident. The story was on all the newscasts and a town meeting was called to talk about the cancer cluster and perhaps hire another lawyer to continue the lawsuit against the chemical company, Dejohn's. Maybe even start a special new cancer clinic in town.

As they were talking, Rebecca joined them on the beach.

"Peter is out of danger," said Rebecca, out of breath and out of anger, "Dad will be picking him up from the hospital this weekend."

"How's his new job at the ice cream packing plant going?" asked Brian.

"It's the first job where he gets a vacation and all the ice cream he can eat. He brought some home last night. Evil Vanilla," laughed Rebecca.

Timi blushed when she realized that Brian had shared their private joke.

"Thank your dad again for recommending him for the job, Brian. How are the treatments going?" asked Rebecca.

"I had my last one yesterday. The doctors say now it's wait and see. Thanks for asking."

Timi blushed again.

I'm like a red traffic light, thought Timi, *first I'm embarrassed and then I'm jealous. But I've never been so happy to have friends surrounding me. Maybe more than friends. Maybe family.*

"Hey, let's go see the sunset by the bay tonight," said Timi, "and make some plans for the rest of the summer."

"Oh no, not another sunset," whined Sataki, and all four of them laughed together. "And Rebecca, don't ask Timi about the weather!"

The talk turned to what their families were doing that weekend and each complained about their family situation.

Pleasure # 15: Making Plans. That night, while watching an end-of-a movie type sunset, their plans included; hospital visits to Peter, writing letters of support to Maria, ice cream eating marathons, town meetings, and research on the harvesting or breeding limits of horseshoe crabs. And, of course, many more sunsets at their favorite spot, now named by the town, Watcher's Bay.

Horseshoe Crabs: More Information

Internet Sites

http://www.njaquarium.org/index.html

http://www.k12.de.us/warner/hscindex.html

http://www.horseshoecrab.org

http://www.beach-net.com/horseshoe/Bayhorsecrab.html

http://www.audubon.org/campaign/horseshoe

http://www.njaudubon.org/Conservation/HSCrabAlert.html

http://sierraactivist.org/article.php?sid=11481

Books

Cannon, Annie and Crenson, Victoria. 2003. *Horseshoe Crabs and Shorebirds: The Story of a Food Web.* Marshall Cavendish Corporation.

Dunlap, Julie. 1999 *Extraordinary Horseshoe Crabs (Nature Watch).* Carolrhoda Books.

Horowitz, Ruth. 2000. *Crab Moon.* Cambridge, MA: Candlewick Press.

Tate, Suzanne. 1991. *Harry the Horseshoe Crab.* Nags Head, NC: Nags Head Art.

ABOUT THE AUTHOR

Terry Moore has been a third grade teacher in Tenafly, NJ for 21 years and lives in Verona, N.J.

He has written for Rethinking Schools Magazine, taught writing process at Columbia University in New York City and created an Environmental Activist Webquest (www.tenafly.k12.nj.us/~tmoore/ webquest/envir.webquest.htm) for elementary school children.

He has a wife, Kim, and a daughter, Kate, who refuses to eat any type of crab.

Mr. Moore believes that environmentalism begins with each individual but must extend to other forces responsible for the environment, like corporations, fisherman, breederies, scientists and the media.

ABOUT THE ILLUSTRATOR

Linda DeLeo is a graphic artist and Senior Education and Training Consultant for Learning and Organizational Development at Ricoh Corporation in Fairfield, N.J. This is her first children's book. She lives in Wayne, NJ.